FROM THE TOP OF A GRAIN ELEVATOR

From the Top of a Grain Elevator

by Barbara Nickel

Illustrated by Kathy Thiessen

An imprint of
Beach Holme Publishing
Vancouver, B.C.

This book is published by Beach Holme Publishing, #226—2040 West
12th Ave., Vancouver, BC, V6J 2G2. This is a Sandcastle Book.

The publisher and author acknowledge the
generous assistance of The Canada Council
and the BC Ministry of Small Business,
Tourism and Culture.

THE CANADA COUNCIL | LE CONSEIL DES ARTS
FOR THE ARTS | DU CANADA
SINCE 1957 | DEPUIS 1957

Editor: Joy Gugeler
Cover Illustration: Kathy Thiessen
Production and Design: Teresa Bubela

Canadian Cataloguing in Publication Data

Nickel, Barbara Kathleen, 1966-
  From the top of a grain elevator

Poems.
(A Sandcastle Book)
ISBN 0-88878-397-3

  1. Prairie Provinces--Juvenile poetry. I. Thiessen, Kathy. II. Title.
PS8577.I3F76 1999   jC811'.54   C99-910314-8
PZ7.N557Fr 1999

For Courtney, Danica, Zoey, Connor and Sophia
and for my father, Arnold Nickel, with gratitude and love

— B.N.

For Nicole, Jacquie, Brad and Bernie with love

— K.T.

Table of Contents

In My Own Tracks

CROCUS HUNT

The Slough Cycle: Spring

At first a trickle
and drip
off the tip
of an icicle.

Then our snowman
topples
into lop-
sided humps we leap-

frog over to see
our slough,
pond of blue
run-off still icy.

A pig's trough
is our boat,
cleared of oats
so we stick-pole across

bringing cream to the
neighbour,
explorers
traversing the deep.

Through the car window,
sloughs glitter
like blue eyes
about to cry

from the wind's tickling,
eyes that
all day watch
the sky's tricks with clouds.

A slough catches sunsets,
slivers
of lightning,
falling stars that land

just under the surface
and rise
up in Spring
flashing secrets.

At slough's edge, willows
gaze at
cows who graze,
their maze of trails,

armies of mosquitoes,
crows (pests!)
making nests
and the two of us

building forts to keep
our kingdom
safe from
frog attacks and spying cats.

Note: In the Canadian prairie provinces, *slough* is pronounced *sloo.*

Gopher Tales

I kneel in the snow
by the gopher's hole.

Seeing one means
I can put away my parka,
toque and scarf, look
for crocus and meadowlark.

Gophers eat crops,
trip horses who stumble into holes.
Grandpa remembers:

Dumped buckets of water
down the hole
and waited,
till sure enough, the pest
popped up. I jumped,
whooped, hollered,
bopped it with a stick.
Government gave me
five cents a tail.

Gopher peeks out,
looks both ways,
runs free
across the frozen field.

I run too, singing
to the wind,
I've caught
the first sign of Spring.

Crocus Hunt

I can't hear the crocus but it hears me
wake up early, slide
into rubber boots, muck
through snow to the ditch.

I can't hear the crocus but it hears me
hop along railroad tracks, pick up
after Winter—green glass, pop cans,
a nickel to make me rich.

I can't hear the crocus but it hears me
search for clues in the thick,
dead grass by the culvert, look
for a pale blue, purplish flower.

I can't hear the crocus but it hears me
with its pointed ears untucked
by Spring and alert as a cat's, their backs
a sun-silvery fuzz I touch

to hear frogs hiccupping
down at the creek, the tiny crack
of a magpie's egg, Spring unpacking
all over the place and the *hush*

of a treasure that listens, all ears.

Songs for Jumping Rope

Snow on the tulips,
 snow on my kite,
all the tiny new leaves
 covered in white.

Snow on the backstop,
 snow in the way,
my ball game cancelled
 by a blizzard in May.

Lunchbag,
lunchbag,
what's inside?

  Saskatoon pie
  and a stale french fry.

Lunchbag,
lunchbag,
what's in there?

  Gooseberry jam
  from last summer's fair.

Lunchbag,
lunchbag,
what does it hold?

  Peanut butter sandwiches
  four years old.

Tent worms, tent worms
 living in the trees,
 in your silky houses,
 eating all the leaves.

Tent worms, tent worms
 turning trees gray,
 take your silky houses
 and move away!

Mud puddle,
 mud puddle,
melting snow and ice puddle,
 try to jump across it
 but don't fall in!

Mud puddle,
 mud puddle,
big, cold and dark puddle,
 Courtney jumps across it
 but—whoops! She's in!

The Wind in May

The wind flings sand in my ears
and eyes, jangles the chains
of the playground swing, sings
down the slide, "You can't escape!"
and bulldozes against
my bike all the way home.

It's blown through the window
to rummage around, puffed
dust on my turtle and my new
microscope. "Enough!" I shout,
but the wind doesn't hear,
scattering my homework pages.

Is this the wind Grandpa fought as a boy,
one that licked scraps of cloud from the sky?

There was no rain for the crops,
just the wind's dry whisper
around the empty silo, dried fish
and white beans from the government
for supper, dust and grit whirling
all night through Grandpa's dreams.

When will it ever keep quiet?
"Never!" our screen door slams.

I get back on my bike,
hold my jacket open like a sail
and the wind whirs behind me, pushes
me past fields stirred into ocean waves,
my jacket flapping, I sail for miles,
the wind a friend at my back.

Spring Recital

Meadowlark Solo

When does the meadowlark wake up,
break the morning with her song?

I walk down the gravel road,
try to snatch it from the dawn.

Her song's too quick for me,
like a quiver or a fawn

or a bird on a telephone pole—
makes me shiver, then is gone.

Magpie Quartet

Squawk!
      Caw!
Cackle!
      Caw!

All day they squabble
from the roof of the barn,

four sore throats
sounding over the farm.

They can't stay together
so I wave my arms, conduct.

Four raw voices
strike the sky's calm:

Caw!   Cackle!
    Squawk!   Caw!

Frog Chorus Round Song

For three voices. A new voice begins with each new stanza. Move clockwise around the circle.

All voices begin here.

—From the dugout, hundreds
of voices croak a round—

—Ribbet, ribbet,
ribbet, ribbet—

—Eerie, hiccuping
sounds slip to dusk
like rain to the pond
fill my ears
with deep green sound—

—Eerie, hiccuping
sounds slip to dusk
like rain to the pond
fill my ears
with deep green sound—

—Ribbet, ribbet,
ribbet, ribbet—

—From the dugout, hundreds
of voices croak a round—

—From the dugout, hundreds
of voices croak a round—

—Ribbet, ribbet,
ribbet, ribbet—

—Eerie, hiccuping
sounds slip to dusk
like rain to the pond
fill my ears
with deep green sound—

TASTING FLOWERS

The Slough Cycle: Summer

June afternoon: we work fractions
on the blackboard, chalk squeaks,
I yawn, my fractions squiggling
down like worms in our slough
that right about now is as drowsy

as a cow, long grass eyelashes
drooping in the heat.
Water striders' legs—quick
pencils sketching *t's* and *w's*
over the surface—put it to sleep

like the chalk numbers I draw
over and over until—
the bell! Short cut across the hay field
and I'm first to wake up the slough,
trample the ooze on the bottom,

feel it squish up between my toes.
Striders clear the way for our races:
front crawl, back crawl, butterfly—
splash, dip, spray. We slip
from the slough and feel its revenge:

scratch our legs all the way home.

At Nemieben Lake

My paddle dips, makes
a small wave ripple the lake,
spread out in circles.
Does it enter the loon's song,
shiver across the pink sky?

Northern Pike wriggles
clear of our shiny, striped hooks,
swishes a secret
to others who swim away.
Red sun cleans our fishless boat.

Dusk smears and smudges,
fingerpaints the sky purple.
Whining in chorus,
swarms of hungry mosquitoes
come down for a lakeside bite.

Driving Home from the Lake

The station wagon hums
a lullaby over the crunch
of gravel as I watch northern lights
swim like hundreds of green minnows.
I'd like to hold one,
try to catch it...

I take my fishing rod,
some peanut butter, snacks,
flippers, snorkel, mask.
I slip through the window,
slide above farms, my arms
pushing away the cold air.

I bait my rod
with toasted marshmallows,
then cast and cast
for northern lights but they dart
into dark caves, slippery
and thin behind stars...

I look out to shadows
of grain elevators,
the lights of town,
the blur of green
behind me, waving
out of reach.

Saskatoons

Saskatoons,
small and wild,
moons of purple-blue
on bushes by the river.

Saskatoons,
sweet and soft, pop
between my teeth,
dribble down my chin.

Saskatoons,
dusty and smooth,
plunk into my pail
with twigs and bugs.

Saskatoons
by late afternoon
turn the bottom
into a Saskatoon sea.

Saskatoons,
sorted and washed,
stirred and squashed
into Saskatoon jam.

Saskatoons
for supper and lunch,
inside me wild moons,
purple-blue by the river.

Constellations

The road between your house and mine's up there.
My best friend's driveway is dusty, cool under
our sunburned legs. She lies back, points to where
the stars, like tiny porch lights, seem to curve
past caraganas on our road. We call
another strip of stars White Ditch—where we
pick baby's-breath, and there are Peas We've Shelled,
Birch Treehouse, Notes of Songs and Burnt Cookies.
I see a road that goes away from here.
Is it that blur of stars like snow, distant
sea foam or tears, lights in our windows years
from now? Will I look out, know where she is?
Tonight our constellations, dot by dot,
hold us to this huge sky, the smell of dust.

Caraganas

My circle of dirt
inside this caragana hedge,
this windbreaker,
dustcatcher,
fence,
leafy screen I peek through
to the park where my friends play ball.

Birds fuss, ants march
across my toes.
I suck caragana flowers,
yellow and sweet as candy.

They play.
I'll stay inside
my hideout of honey and dust.

The caragana is our backstop.
It hides softballs like bubblegum
in its fat, green cheeks.

At dusk, the game over,
we make whistles
from the caragana pods—
peel them open, bite off the ends,
send our songs to the sky.

*

Dad chopped down the caraganas,
called them a nuisance
and wild, planted new,
fancy hedges in their place.

But he didn't get the roots.

In a corner of our yard
I've found the caragana's knobbly bones.
Someday I'll make whistles
and hideouts,
taste flowers again.

June Thunderstorm

The dust whispers to the grass,
grass to lilacs,
lilacs to wind,
wind to sparrows.

But the sparrows can't keep a secret,
I hear them chattering
in the tangled vines
by my window.

The sky's face is grimy
with dark clouds, voice rumbling
through town like an old truck,
eyes blinking silver
over the grain elevators.

Rain drowns the thirsty secrets
of dust and grass and lilacs,
runs rivers down their throats,

shivers down my back
as I sit on the bed watching,
nose pressed against the window.

Later, everything is greener,
dripping in the quiet, evening light,
listening to the sky's distant grumbles
like a hungry stomach in church.

A hush—
then a sparrow sings
her summer secrets.

Northern Lights

The sky is restless tonight,
twists and turns
in eerie green sheets,
shifting and rolling,
shimmering
above fields of wheat.

The sky is restless tonight,
throws off her dark quilt
with its pattern of stars.
Her dreams tremble and sing,
green lights wavering
until she wakes, yawns: dawn.

The Town & Country Fair

I've waited all summer
to hear cows in the park,
softballs in leather gloves,
music over loudspeakers.

The Giant Parade:
pink-tissue floats,
bagpipes, drums,
horses with ribbons
and clowns honking noses.

Pancakes in sun-melted butter,
cotton candy, sunflower seeds,
salty shells I spit
from the bleachers.

Prize ruby raspberries
and pickles on display,
the lights of town, sugar sprinkles
I could scoop in my hand
as I swoop to the sky
on the ferris wheel.

Fireworks: bursting, crackling
spattering green, pink
and orange streaks
that fade into the night.

Now the air seems colder,
the fair over,
summer almost gone.

NIGHT HARVEST

The Slough Cycle: Fall

Glint of silver in the cattails—
Winter bit last night.
Willow leaves know it, drifting
yellow on the slough.

Mallards know it too, nose-diving
for food, pretending
they won't have to leave. Silence
hovers—a breath

Fall takes before jumping
the barbed wire fence to Winter.
Blackbirds rise up from the bush,
begin their journey.

Night Harvest

High in the combine,
brothers left behind,
just Dad and I
rumble up and down

rows of wheat, race
to cut our crop
before the rain,
headlights pushing the dark.

Dad shows me switches, dials,
the tiny window
where I watch grain pour,
hear it roar like a waterfall.

We eat jam sandwiches,
talk, sing rounds,
after-bedtime hours
wind behind us like straw.

Tonight I share Dad
only with the moon, whose
long, milky hand stretches the field,
pulls it before us to dawn.

Up With the Grain

Today I watched them knock
our town's grain elevator down.

Cloud of dust, pile of rubble
where it once stood
like a white, wooden soldier
beside the railroad tracks,
Melthern in black across its middle.

Now they'll haul the grain
to a huge, cement tower
nothing like the shoulders
that sloped above town,
musty and dark inside

where a bright green engine putted
as it lifted kernels up the elevator
shaft to bins at the peak. I wanted
to rise up with the grain
and the swallows.

From that high window
I'd see blue squares
of flax, sloughs
like jewels, knots of bush,
roads to explore for miles.

Today our elevator disappeared
but my view is still here, clearing with the dust.

From the Top of a Grain Elevator

```
        rye      oats wheat canola peas barley
     wheat      rye barley rye flax wheat rye
    flax beans      flax corn sorghum peas wheat
  canola  barley     oats flax wheat canola beans rye
```

```
  wheat oats peas    wheat rye flax oats barley wheat
  oats corn flax rye  rye flax oats barley lentil sorghum
  wheat oats barley  wheat rye      up here      barley
  canola flax beans  barley flax   I can see     wheat
  sorghum oats rye   corn oats   the whole world beans
   barely flax canola   peas rye barley corn oats wheat
  wheat corn oats rye    sorghum wheat beans rye canola
    peas canola lentil corn
   oats rye wheat wheat barley       flax peas canola flax barley rye
  corn oats rye wheat wheat rye       sorghum peas lentil barley peas
 beans flax canola wheat barley corn    peas lentil wheat oats flax wheat
 beans wheat flax oats peas oats rye   oats lentil rye flax flax canola lentil
 sorghum peas oats canola rye peas     wheat barley flax peas oats canola
 oats canola rye peas oats canola rye   rye peas oats canola rye peas oats
 peas  sorghum beans flax wheat        canola rye peas sorghum beans
 barley beans flax canola oats lentil   flax wheat barley rye beans canola
 flax flax canola wheat flax oats peas  oats lentil flax wheat flax oats peas
 oats sorghum wheat flax rye corn       oats sorghum rye corn flax lentil
 flax lentils flax rye corn barley flax  flax rye corn barley flax wheat
 wheat lentil rye peas beans barley    lentil peas beans barley oats corn
 oats corn barley lentil flax corn peas  barley lentil flax corn peas wheat
 wheat barley oats peas lentil oats     corn barley oats peas lentil oats
 beans flax rye canola wheat barley     beans flax rye canola wheat barley
 beans lentil sorghum barley barley    beans sorghum wheat barley corn
 corn lentil rye wheat barley· oats     lentil rye wheat barley oats peas
 peas lentil sorghum canola wheat      barley sorghum canola wheat beans
 beans rye beans rye canola lentil      rye canola lentil peas oats rye bean
 peas oats beans peas lentil sorghum   peas lentil rye sorghum barley wheat
 barley rye wheat wheat beans flax rye  wheat beans flax rye oats barley flax
 oats barley flax rye canola oats peas  canola rye oats peas wheat sorghum
 barley wheat barley lentil canola flax  barley lentil rye wheat barley oats peas
 wheat  rye canola lentil corn rye oats  lentil sorghum flax canola wheat beans
 lentil beans rye canola lentil sorghum  canola lentil rye wheat barley oats rye
```

October

Piles of burning leaves
  fill the town with spicy smoke,
    scent my new jacket,
      wool socks on the line, my hair.
      Jack o' lanterns light the air.

      I wait near the tracks
     for the train to rattle by.
   A blast, iron cry
  the grass remembers, quivers
long after the train has passed.

Tiny, fiery
  crabapples scattered in grass.
    They taste furious,
   sour faces falling from the tree.
I scowl too, fill my pockets.

At Batoche

Did they ride in these hills,
Louis Riel, the Métis,
hide behind this willow bluff,
over a hundred years ago?

Did they hear this prairie wind,
listen for danger from the East,
marching soldiers, bagpipes, guns,
over a hundred years ago?

Did they stand in this poplar shadow,
remember fiddles and nights of dance,
miss their quiet farms and peace,
over a hundred years ago?

Did they scout this Saskatchewan River,
look for Middleton and his troops,
the prow of a boat beyond the bend,
over a hundred years ago?

Did they feel this scratchy thistle
in the trenches, crouching low,
loading rifles, waiting, waiting,
over a hundred years ago?

Did their hearts race like mine?
Did they shiver? Did they pray
at the Battle of Batoche,
over a hundred years ago?

The Chase

three yellow leaves crouch

    curl & crinkle

        by my feet

the wind sweeps them dancing

                down the street

                               s   c   u   t   t   l

I chase behind   watch them   e

            k i

         s   p   s

                            w

                             i

                           r

                      l

          shuffle

the wind stops for a breath
I crunch one
under my shoe   the wind

                whisks them off

we

      s   g   & s

    w i n   k

              i

            t

             t

           e

            r   the six blocks to school

Buried

I
rake them
higher than the
wheelbarrow run
fast jump in leaves tickling
my neck scoop up handfuls of
wrinkled dark orange and purple red
cover my head in smells of dirt and dew
and dust peek out spy on crow and cat burst
free like laughter crow flies away cat licks my
feet while I rake them higher than the wheelbarrow

Prairie Halloween

I want to be a ballerina
with a pink tutu, soft matching slippers,
tiara, clip-on earrings,
pink nail polish, thin tights
and NO SLEEVES!

I want to be a hummingbird
with ruby throat and silver wings,
tiny and delicate,
flitting from house to house
collecting treats like nectar.

I want to be a deep sea diver
with wetsuit, flippers, mask, tank,
schools of tropical fish
floating all around me,
attached with invisible wires.

Halloween Rule #1:

Your costume must be big enough to fit over your
    snowmobile suit.

Halloween Rule #2:

If it snows, you have to wear your mitts, boots and toque.

A pink tutu over a snowmobile suit?
A hummingbird flitting in clunky old boots?
A deep sea diver in a pompom toque?

It begins in wisps,
just a few flakes
threading my brother's goblin hair,
then the whole block's a flurry.
Peaks form on the cardboard brims
of witch hats, magic wands
flash like Christmas lights
but I'm warm inside my snowsuit-tutu
as my pillowcase fills up
with candy and snow.

IN MY OWN TRACKS

The Slough Cycle: Winter

Crossovers, zigzags,
crack-the-whip and six-toothed
star—our blades
scrape messages to the moon
on the frozen slough.

Bumps under my skates
and even though it's night
I see moonlit bubbles
and bugs move
beneath the ice.

What else is trapped there?
August sun, our footprints
in the mud,
Grandpa's voice, laughing,
fifty springs ago?

"You're it!" he tags me—
now it's my turn to skate
past skidoo tracks
in stubble fields
tumbled with stars.

Up there the moon's frozen,
a slough traced
with games of tag,
circles and circles
each year in the cold.

Gift

Last night the sky crocheted
an afghan for our town.

This blue dawn
she tucks us in,
folding the delicate edge
around the corners
of the curling rink
across the street.

We pull on our boots,
dance shrieking out
to the yard in our pajamas,
feel the gift in our hands,
under our feet.

I lift my face,
it kisses my forehead
with one
        lacy
           flake.

❉

On the dark walk
across the park to school,
I breathe into my scarf
to warm my face, sink
to my knees with each step.

I want to stay,
alone in the deep,
silent snow, alone
in my own tracks,
not there yet.

*

I lie down on the snow
on the way home from school,
feel the cold on my arms
and backs of my legs, move
them back and forth
to make perfect angel wings,
snow sneaking under my mitts
to sting my wrists.

I try to stand
but fall back
to rest on my angel
with the crooked wing.

Facewash

On a brittle afternoon,
I walk home in the middle
of the road, ears covered with mitts.

My brother sneaks up,
rubs a handful of snow
in my face—it trickles
like an icy brook to the crook
of my warm belly button.

I grab some snow but he's too far ahead,
running backwards, laughing
as my snowball
falls to pieces.

I want to shove him in drifts,
ambush him,
launch an icy attack.

But by the time I catch up,
my anger has melted.

Hoarfrost

Who iced the trees last night?
Skinny grey branches turned
white and thick,
ghostly bearded trunks.

Who iced the telephone wire last night?
Black snake decorated
with fancy lace,
torn fringe drifting down.

Who iced my bike last night?
Chain and sprockets starred
with frost, the grease
and dirt disguised.

Who iced the sparrow's nest last night?
Twigs and grass spread
with a clean blanket,
covering scraps and vines.

Who iced the ends of my sister's hair?
Eyelashes crusted,
toque dusted with sugar
as she skates on the dugout rink.

Hockey Game

I escaped from the house
without a toque.
Now my ears are numb,
but I don't care. All my friends
are toqueless too.

Julie's got new jeans, Kate's hair is orange,
my ski jacket looks dumb, my hair looks weird,
Melissa likes Randy, Sue is mad at Jill.

Duck!
Watch out for the puck!

Go Wheatkings Go!
Go Wheatkings Go!
Pound the board till your hands tingle,
Go Wheatkings Go!

End of the period.
In the smoky lobby, crowds
line up for hot chocolate and french fries
dripping grease, ketchup, vinegar.

Back on the bleachers
I wish it was over,
can't hear Julie's secrets,
Kate turns her back.

I walk home alone,
rub my ears,
watch the stars.

Forty Below

Long underwear (two pair),
undershirt, T-shirt, turtleneck, sweater,
ski pants, wool socks (two pair),
toque, mitts, boots, parka,
a long scarf Mom winds
around and around until only
my eyes peek through.

I run outside
inside these layers,
hidden from Forty Below.

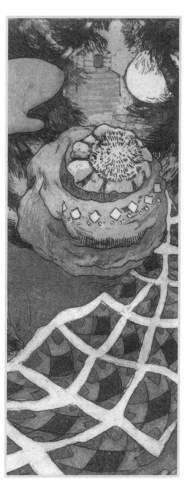

It catches me
with each breath:
dives into my lungs,
numbs the tips of my ears,
nips the bare spot
that Mom forgot.

I look up, wonder
how Forty Below can sharpen
the stars, darken the air,
deepen, whiten the snow.

Wonder how on the coldest night
I feel so warm,
so light I could fly,
tag the tops of pines,
church spire, chimney smoke
hung across the sky.

Getting the Tree

My
whole family,
even our old dog,
trudges to the creek
to find a Christmas tree,
down a snowy slope thick with
willow and rose hip, aspen and spruce.
We run on the ice creek that the beavers
split-level, scout the bank for a perfect tree.
Too skinny, too short, crooked top, branches missing—
after hours we take the lopsided one I found
and search for kindling, make a fire. In woodsmoke that
stays on my parka for days we roast wieners (forgot the ketchup
again!) and marshmallows, drink hot chocolate from a thermos,
haul our tree up the steep bank. Dad carries the dog to the top
where fields have turned a spooky blue. It's called
entre chien et loup,
between dog and
wolf, a magic time
that isn't day and
isn't night, but dusk.

Glossary

Battle of Batoche: Batoche, located in the province of Saskatchewan, was the site of the Northwest Rebellion of 1885, a battle between the Métis, led by Louis Riel and Gabriel Dumont, and the Canadian troops, led by General Middleton.

Caragana: A type of hedge commonly found in the Canadian prairie provinces, originally planted in fields as a windbreak.

Dugout: A human-made pond, used for irrigation purposes on farms.

Northern Pike: A large, slender, fresh-water fish that has a long, flat snout.

Saskatoon: Berries to be found often in ravines of the prairies.

Slough (pronounced sloo): A natural marshy or reedy pool, often found along the fields of the prairies.

Water Strider: Insects that have long, slender legs fringed with hairs, allowing them to dart about on the surface of water.

About Barbara Nickel

Barbara Nickel's young adult novel *The Secret Wish of Nannerl Mozart* was shortlisted for the Mr. Christie Book Award, the Geoffrey Bilson Award and the Red Cedar Award. Her adult poetry *The Gladys Elegies* won the 1997 Pat Lowther Award. Her poem "Night Harvest", included in *From the Top of a Grain Elevator,* received Honourable Mention in the B.C. Federation of Writers Literary Rites "Writing for Children" Contest in 1994.

Barbara Nickel holds an M.F.A. in Creative Writing from the University of British Columbia, where she was the poetry editor of *Prism international* and has also instructed writing classes. She lives in St. John's, Newfoundland.

Author's Note

While writing the poems in *From the Top of a Grain Elevator*, I experimented with lots of different forms. To write the poems in "The Slough Cycle", for example, I used a form called *syllable-count meter*. In this form, you assign a set number of syllables for each line in a stanza, then repeat that pattern throughout the poem. In "The Slough Cycle: Spring", a poem with four-line stanzas, the first line is five syllables, the second is two syllables, the third line is three syllables and the fourth line is five syllables.

The poems in "At Nemieben Lake" and "October" use the *tanka* form, which is another type of syllable-count poem. This is a Japanese form consisting of thirty-one syllables, arranged in five lines, each of seven syllables, except the first and third, which each have five syllables.

I've used lots of rhyme patterns in the poems, sometimes at the ends of lines, but often in a less structured way inside the lines. When making up rhymes, I don't always use *full rhyme* (that/cat). I also use something called *half-rhyme*, or *slant-rhyme*. Half-rhymes in which just the vowels of two words are the same (trough/across) are called *assonance*. Rhymes where just the last consonants are the same (realm/from) are called *consonance*.

"Constellations" is one kind of *sonnet*. This form is divided into three *quatrains*, or sections of four lines each, and a section of two lines called a *couplet*. The rhyming pattern for this type of sonnet is as follows: *abab cdcd efef gg*. It also uses a *meter*, or rhythm called *iambic pentameter*. This is made by putting weak beats and strong beats into units called *feet*. An *iambic foot* is a weak beat (˘) followed by a strong beat (/). Five iambic feet together is called iambic pentameter:

˘ / ˘ / ˘ / ˘ / ˘ /
The road be tween your house and mine's up there.

"Buried", "From the Top of a Grain Elevator", and "Getting the Tree" are called *shaped poems*, which means that they take the shape of the poem's subject.

A form is like a container for a poem. Once I set it up, I often vary the original pattern, depending on what I feel the poem needs. For example, I allowed the syllable count patterns in "The Slough Cycle" poems to change on many lines. In "Constellations", I used half-rhyme for almost the entire sonnet pattern. In that poem, I played with the iambic pentameter rhythm by reversing weak beats and strong beats, or replacing a regular foot with two strong beats. I try to use a form without letting it get in the way of what I want to say.

I grew up—from birth to high school graduation and summers beyond—in Rosthern, a town in Saskatchewan. Even after I moved away and lived in many different places, I always felt that Rosthern was my home, and I needed to gather up the sights, smells, sounds and events of my growing up years and turn them into poems so that I wouldn't lose that home. Hockey games and the Town & Country Fair were events that returned year after year like the yellow bloom of caragana and the first fall of snow. The seasons cycled around like the ferris wheel and my father's stories of sloughs and gopher hunting. I always thought the grain elevators must watch it all. They couldn't miss a thing—they seemed so tall. Now they're going extinct. This book's a bit of what I think they saw.

About Kathy Thiessen

Kathy Thiessen studied art at the University of Manitoba, Banff School of Fine Arts, and the University of Saskatchewan, where she graduated with a Bachelor of Fine Arts Degree. She has had several solo exhibitions and has had experience in scenic painting for theatrical productions. Kathy grew up on a farm near MacGregor, Manitoba, and has remained a prairie resident all her life. She has lived in Rosthern, a small Saskatchewan town, since 1971. She was one of the founders of Station Arts Centre in Rosthern in 1990, for which she received the national L'escarbot award in 1992. Thiessen is currently the Arts Administrator and Curator of the Centre, and teaches art at Rosthern Junior College.

Illustrator's Note

The process of illustrating for *From the Top of a Grain Elevator* by Barbara Nickel has been a profound and enlightening experience for me. First of all, as I sketched and articulated my ideas in the initial stages of the project, I found myself identifying with so many experiences in these beautiful poems. It gave me a renewed appreciation for the true spirit of the prairies. Furthermore, the line/aquatint etching medium gave me the opportunity to explore details and subject matter that have always been important in my life. Elements of rhythm, pattern, colour and motion all become a dynamic and vital part of the overall composition, as they do in music. The leaves dance, the flowers laugh, the sloughs awaken and the wheatfields sing. Through the use of repetitious motifs, I have attempted to capture the essence of prairie life through the eyes of a child. Each season, each cycle, and each place, is wrapped with a quilt of endless experiences. The elevator floats in each sky, watching and waiting. . . . This book captures the magical moment that every age can relive and enjoy! Thank you Barb and Joy for this unique and wonderful opportunity.

Acknowledgements

For invaluable assistance and support, the author would like to thank Sue Ann Alderson, the 1992/93 and 1993/94 Writing for Children workshops at the University of British Columbia, the University of B.C.'s Department of Creative Writing and the Graduate Fellowship fund, Joy Gugeler, Beach Holme Publishing, Alison Acheson, Annette LeBox, Gayle Friesen, Christy Dunsmore, Caroline Davis Goodwin, Shannon Stewart, Stephanie Bolster, Arnold Nickel, Lorene Nickel, Hank Nickel, Carrie MacDonald, Kathy Thiessen, Erin Cox, Tim Nickel, Cindy Nickel, Karen Alden, Trevor Janzen, David Voth, Mary Voth and Bevan Voth.